Harry's Party

Chris Powling
and Scoular Anderson

Collins

To my Mum   **CP**

Look out for more *Jets* from Collins

Jessy Runs Away • *Best Friends* • **Rachel Anderson**
Changing Charlie • *Clogpots in Space* • **Scoular Anderson**
Ivana the Inventor • *Ernest the Heroic Lion Tamer* • **Damon Burnard**
Two Hoots • *Almost Goodbye Guzzler* • **Helen Cresswell**
Shadows on the Barn • **Sarah Garland**
Nora Bone • *The Mystery of Lydia Dustbin's Diamonds* • **Brough Girling**
Thing on Two Legs • *Thing in a Box* • **Diana Hendry**
Desperate for a Dog • *More Dog Trouble* • **Rose Impey**
Georgie and the Dragon • *Georgie and the Planet Raider* • **Julia Jarman**
Cowardy Cowardy Cutlass • *Free With Every Pack* • **Robin Kingsland**
Mossop's Last Chance • *Mum's the Word* • **Michael Morpurgo**
Hiccup Harry • *Harry Moves House* • *Harry's Party* • *Harry the Superhero* •
Harry With Spots On • **Chris Powling**
Rattle and Hum, Robot Detectives • **Frank Rodgers**
Our Toilet's Haunted • **John Talbot**
Rhyming Russell • *Messages* • **Pat Thomson**
Monty the Dog Who Wears Glasses • *Monty's Ups and Downs* • **Colin West**
Ging Gang Goolie, it's an Alien • *Stone the Crows, it's a Vacuum Cleaner* •
Bob Wilson

First published by A & C Black Ltd in 1989
Published by Collins in 1989

Collins is an imprint of HarperCollins*Publishers*Ltd,
77–85 Fulham Palace Road, Hammersmith, London W6 8JB

ISBN 978-0-00-6733478

Text © Chris Powling 1989
Illustrations © Scoular Anderson 1989

The author and the illustrator assert the moral right to
be identified as the author and the illustrator of the work.
A CIP record for this title is available from the British Library.

Are you keen on parties?

I am.

Or I was, rather. After what happened at my last party, I'm not so sure.

And don't tell me it was all my own
fault, because I've heard that already
from plenty of other kids.

They won't let me forget it, not *ever*.

It all started with the invitation to Mandy's party.

come to a
SPOOK PARTY

At ..... Mandy's .....

On Saturday 15th April

At ..... 4.30 pm .....
please wear fancy dress

I decided to go as a vampire.

'Why a vampire?' asked my mum.

7

She still helped me make a terrific costume.

The party was terrific, too . . .

. . . except when the other kids
ganged up on me.

Then I got an invitation from Winston.

Come to a...
PIRATE PARTY
in fancy dress
at: ...Winston's
on 28th May 3.30

I decided to go as Blackbeard.

13

The costume she helped me make
this time was even better, though.

It was a great party . . .

. . . even if I wasn't too keen on the way it ended.

When Sareeka's invitation arrived,
I knew at once who I wanted to be.

Sareeka
invites you to a
COPS AND ROBBERS
PARTY

AT 3.00 pm
ON July 20th

'Robocop?' said Mum. 'Why do you want to go as Robocop?'

'He's half-cop and half-robot, Mum. In a film I saw advertised on TV, he goes round zapping everybody really hard!'

She did, too.

At Sareeka's party I had a
smashing, zap-happy time . . .

. . . till everyone else suddenly lost their tempers.

What was the matter with them, I wondered? Was I the only kid left in the world who knew how to enjoy a party?

Serve them right if I tore up the next
invitation I got. Yes – that's what
I'd do.

And when they came round to my
house to beg me to change my mind,
I'd make them wait for ages before I did.

The trouble was, there weren't any more invitations. Was this because there weren't any more parties?

'That must be it,' I told Mum.
'I mean, they wouldn't leave me out on purpose.'

'Wouldn't they?' said Mum.

'Maybe there's another reason,
Harry. For instance, did you behave
yourself at those other parties
you went to?'

What was she on about?

Hadn't I made certain the other parties were fun?

Why blame me if the other kids got over-excited and had tantrums?

So I was really fed up when I heard a crowd of kids in the playground talking about Tracey's Stone Age Party.

'When was this?' I asked.

They just laughed and ran off.

A week later, when I was walking back from the fish and chip shop with Dad, I passed Roger's house.

It was full of kids having a Disco Party.

But I did really. I wanted to bash up
every kid who was there, Roger
especially.

Worst of all, though, was
Samantha's Cinema Party.
Her parents had fixed up
a big screen in their
living room,

with a proper projector, proper
tickets to let you in . . .

ABC CINEMA
No 005763 ADMIT ONE
SCREEN ONE

and proper ice-cream and pop-corn in the interval.

I heard about all this during a wet lunchtime at school. Every kid in my class was describing how they'd been asked to turn up dressed as their favourite film-character.

So why not me?
Wasn't I a genius
at livening-up
parties?

In this case I'd
have gone as
Godzilla,
or maybe
King Kong,

and pulled down
the screen on top
of everybody
when the movie
was over.
An ace finish, yes?
Except I never got
the chance to do it.

Why not? Jealousy,
that's why not.
The other kids
couldn't stand my
bright ideas and
brilliant costumes,

so they'd left me
out. Honestly,
how mean
can you get?

Of course, I wasn't
going to let them get
away with it. I'd make
them an offer they
couldn't refuse.
Mum and Dad would
help me, I knew.

POP!

INVITATION

TO

Harry's

OUTER SPACE

PARTY

DARE YOU COME?

ON 8th October
AT 5.00 pm

P.S. my Mum and Dad
will be next door

'What do you mean, "DARE" we come along?' everyone asked.

'Scaredy-cats can stay away,' I said.

Naturally, no one said no after that.

No one was late, either.

Mum and Dad had really worked
hard, I must admit. Our front room
was so much like a space-station,
I hardly recognised it.

All the food had an outer-space look
as well, and the music we played
was so spooky it sounded as if it was
being beamed from the other side of
the universe.

To my surprise, they didn't argue
one bit.

The instant they'd gone, I nipped
upstairs to change into my costume.

This was my best ever.

It was just perfect for paying back all my so-called mates.

They'd get the shock of their lives

when I burst

into the

living room

dressed as . . .

Don't ask me what happened next.
It was as if they'd planned
the whole thing.

Before I could even blink, I was tied up
like a parcel in my own alien costume,
with my mask turned back-to-front
so I couldn't see a thing!

'Well, well,' came Mandy's voice.
'If it isn't Harry, the party wrecker!'

And that's just what they did –
except it wasn't just the party
decorations that copped it. From all
the different noises, I could tell
what they were up to . . .

. . . soaking the carpet with
orange squash . . .

. . . tearing up books from the
bookcase . . .

. . .breaking up the furniture . . .

. . . ripping seat-covers . . .

. . . and duffing up the television set!

But it only made them worse.

'That's it,' Mandy said. 'Well done, gang. It's the worst mess I've ever seen – as if a whole herd of Harrys had ruined all our parties at once.'

I was too upset to fight back. They bundled me upstairs to my own bedroom . . .

and dumped me under the covers,
alien costume and all.

The front door banged shut
behind them.

I lay there for hours and hours,
picturing the scene in the living room.

I was so scared, I reckon I *shivered*
myself out of the alien costume.

What would Mum and Dad say
when they came back?

Then I heard their voices in the hall. I held my breath.

And held it . . .

. . . and held it . . .

. . . till I nearly burst.

Why was it all so quiet?

Eventually, I couldn't stand it any longer. I tiptoed down the stairs

and pressed my ear flat against the door of the living room.

Was that the noise of the television?
How could it be the television,
when I knew it was smashed to bits?

I took a gulp of air and pushed open the door.

It was true. I'd never seen the room looking so spick-and-span. Nothing was broken.

Nothing was out of place. Nothing was even *dusty*.

I stood there, gob-smacked. How had they done it?

But I had a nasty idea they were giggling at something else.

There was a lot of giggling at school next day, too. Also a lot of sound-effects.

Sound-effects?

I felt a real wally, I can tell you. The only thing that cheered me up was an invitation to Desmond's Zoo Party.

I'm going to go as a tortoise!